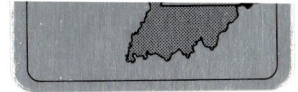

E.S.E.A. Chapter 2 1995
Clay Community Schools

INCREDIBLY

by
Catherine Bousquet

Series director :
François Cherrier

HIDDEN

new Discovery
B·O·O·K·S
New York

Beyond appearances

1

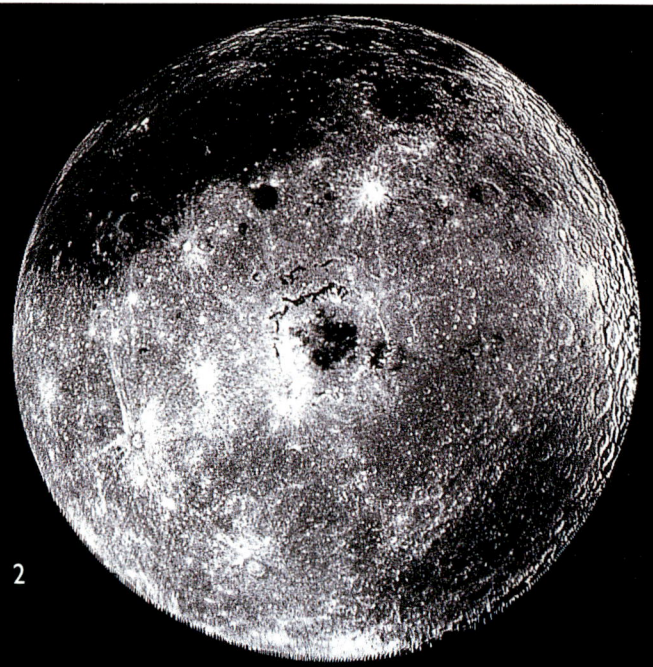

2

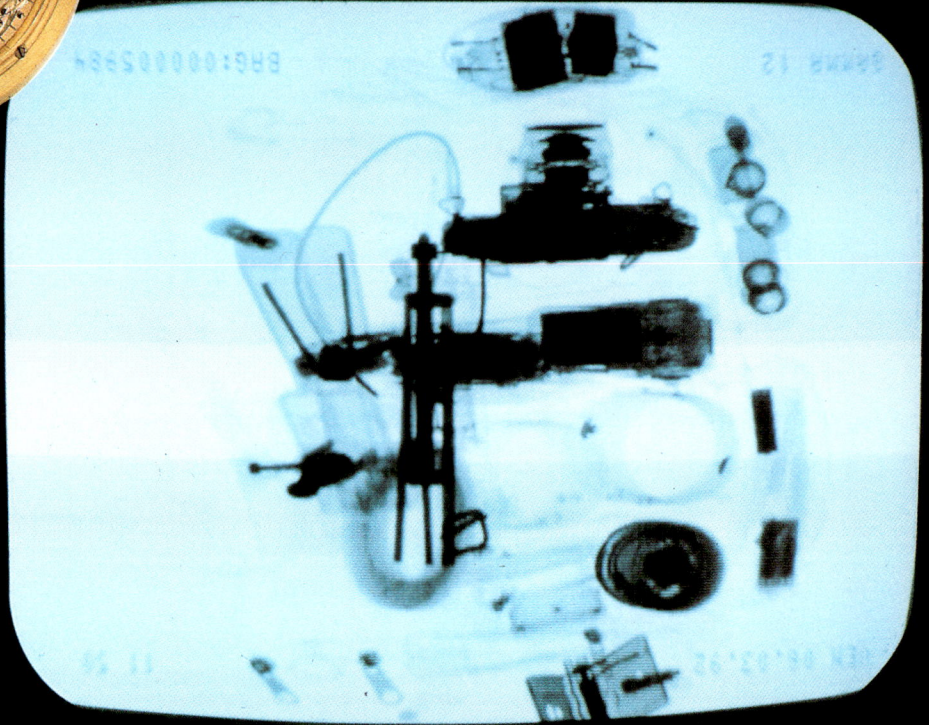

3

The world surrounding us has unseen facets, just like the dark side of the moon. The countless external images reflect an infinite number of unseen realities, all unsuspected, unpredictable, and imperceptible. Yet we cannot see beyond the surface of things. Nature's tricks—in the form of protective coverings, opaque barriers, rigid shells, and a multitude of other devices—are all obstacles beyond which the human eye cannot see. What would it be like to have another set of eyes that could slip through the cracks of reality for a closer look? A dream? No. The visible appears in a new light and the invisible becomes clear, merely by changing our point of view or using the sophisticated eyes of technology. A strange procession of odd shapes and colors then emerge, revealing the world of the incredibly hidden.

4

5

How can we discover the unknown and strange worlds that lie behind the external appearance of natural or man-made objects? Sometimes, all it takes is to change our point of view, with or without technical assistance, to view this transformation of reality. And the results can be surprising: (1) the dark side of the moon, (2) the inside of a watch case, (3) the inside of a fish egg, (4) a piece of luggage under an X ray, (5) the heart of a stone. These are the metamorphoses of our reality, as surprising as the emergence of a chrysalis (6).

6

The world stripped bare

There's no need for sophisticated equipment to reveal the animal, vegetable, mineral, and even mechanical marvels our world holds yet is reluctant to reveal. Dig, scratch, scrape, peel, lift up, remove, cut, and disassemble: There are many ways to help the eye detect the hiddenmost secrets. Beyond the tricks, wiles, and stratagems displayed by nature lies a remarkable logic and an admirable intelligence. A marvelous complexity is concealed behind the apparent simplicity. At this level, everything is order and beauty.

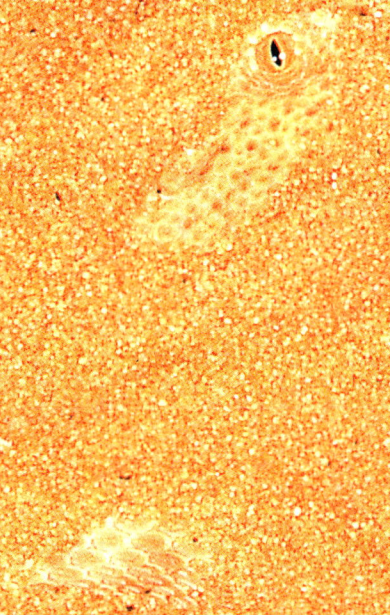

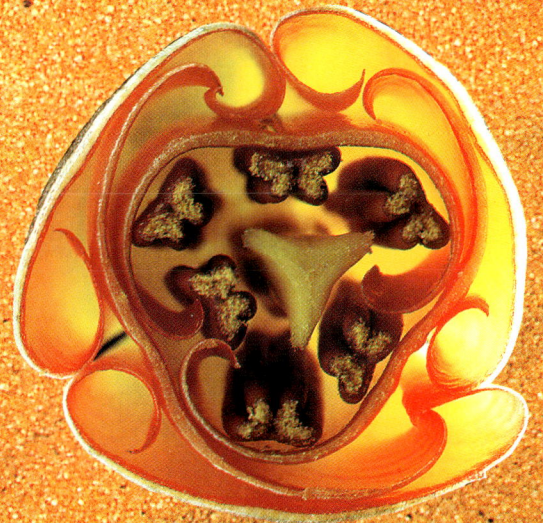

The Sahara viper, coiled
under the sand to escape
the sun, creates artistic,
meandering designs.
A tulip bud, cut in half,
reveals its subtle internal
architecture.

SHELTERS FROM SCRAPS

The world has gone topsy-turvy! Nests are usually in the air; here we see them in the water or on the ground. And if there's a nest, shouldn't a bird be nearby? Not necessarily; this distinction doesn't matter to the male stickleback (called the three-spine stickleback) when its primary concern is to escape from prying eyes. Part of the Gasterosteidae family, it is found in fresh or salt water throughout the Northern Hemisphere. The male of this species is the nest builder! He collects plant fragments that are held together by a threadlike secretion from his kidneys. His motive? After building

The three-spine stickleback, named for its spiny dorsal fins, is a remarkable builder: The precious eggs are well hidden and protected from predators.

his aquatic nest, he performs a courtship dance to entice the female inside, where she lays her eggs. He then enters the nest to fertilize them. Her work is finished: In this species, the male takes charge of the eggs, fanning them with his fins for about six days. He also watches over the freshly hatched young fish.

The Celebes hornbill, native to Indonesia, has an unusual method of nesting. After courtship, the male and female find a tree cavity and together create an impregnable nest. She creates a solid mortar that consists of mud provided by the male, mixed with saliva and droppings. The female remains in her fortress throughout the incubation period, 30 to 50 days, during which the male provides her with food, passing fruits and berries through a slit in the walled-up nest. The young remain in the nest up to four months after birth, well protected from predators. The female will use her solid beak to break through her protective wall if the male does not arrive in time.

A PAINTING UNDER THE BARK

Between the tree and the bark lies a beautiful creation. The artist? The small bark beetle, also known as the "engraver beetle." His medium? The new wood of the epicea, the common spruce tree. These wood engravers live off the tree, but leave behind a unique trace of their passage. The burrowing of the untiring mandibles create astonishing bas-reliefs, works that would be a credit to any modern art museum. The characteristic signature of one leaves indelible scars on the tree: The bark has been transformed into a vast tableau.

You have to look closely to detect the minuscule creator of these designs on the giant trunk of the spruce tree: The bark beetles are less than one-third of an inch long. Yet despite this handicap, they are anatomically well suited to their task. Their cylindrical bodies, covered with long hair, and well-designed grooved elytrons clear their path and help to remove the bark excavated by the insects as they progress through the bark. The females and larvae create vertical and right-angle tunnels, while the males break through new tunnels and hollow out galleries.

In the area between the bark and the edge of the annual growth rings of the wood lies a thin layer of cells called the cambium, which is the formative layer of the plant. This layer forms the year's growth, thus creating the growth rings. It is, unfortunately, also the favorite food of the beetles. Burrowing through the wood, the beetles excavate long galleries. The female beetle lays dozens of eggs that she places in tiny notches at regular intervals. As soon as the larvae hatch, they move away from the "brood gallery." They eat their way out of the tree, consuming wood, cambium, and bark. They finally emerge through a hole about the size of a bullet hole; this is why they are also known as "shot-hole borers."

A collective work: the tattoos of the spruce trees

There's strength in numbers for the bark beetles, which belong to the family Scolytidae. They unerringly detect a weak or sick spruce tree and attack in force. The early stages of their labors leave no more than minuscule marks as they first enter the bark. Gradually, the multitude of insect miners breaks down the system of carefully bored tunnels in which the female lays her eggs. At the end of their work is a chaotic "traffic jam." The entire bark has been transformed into an engraving, a strange landscape with unique, torturous designs. As the breeding season ends, the larvae become pupae and emerge through a final hole in the bark, leaving behind a fascinating work of nature.

ART THAT GETS UNDER THE SKIN

They were cousins. Born the same year—1732—in the same town in southern France—Grasse. But only one of them holds a prominent place in history for his scenes of gallantry and pictures of young, gracious women with fresh complexions and rosy cheeks: Jean-Honoré Fragonard. The other Fragonard, however, was also an artist. But he preferred to depict what the body looks like under the skin.

Anatomical models, which reveal the bones and muscles under the skin, are grisly reminders of school years. They occupied a place of honor in natural history classes, revealing the flat layers of muscles and rivers of veins. Nevertheless, they were made of only harmless papier-mâché or plastic. Honoré Fragonard's creatures, which for centuries have stared out of vacant eyes, are something else altogether: real men and real animals. These are the raw materials used by this surgeon, a professor of anatomy at the Veterinary School in 1762. As the inspired creator of a new "artistic anatomy," a subject that was usually studied using plaster molds or wax figures, Fragonard followed a singular idea, one quite foreign to a purely didactic depiction.

His work did not consist of montages, drawings, engravings, or diagrams: Honoré Fragonard worked with material that was once alive. Human beings and animals were the only way to obtain trustworthy information. They provided a lesson in life and instruction in death. In the intimacy of his office, he prepared dozens of pieces according to his vision, working diligently with original tissue, inventing compositions, searching for effects, even at the risk of losing himself, losing his job, and even losing his sanity. Honoré Fragonard challenged all the taboos of his period. At that time the laws against the appropriation of corpses were strict, and he was surrounded by suspicion and disapproval. He withstood all opposition. Dismissed from the

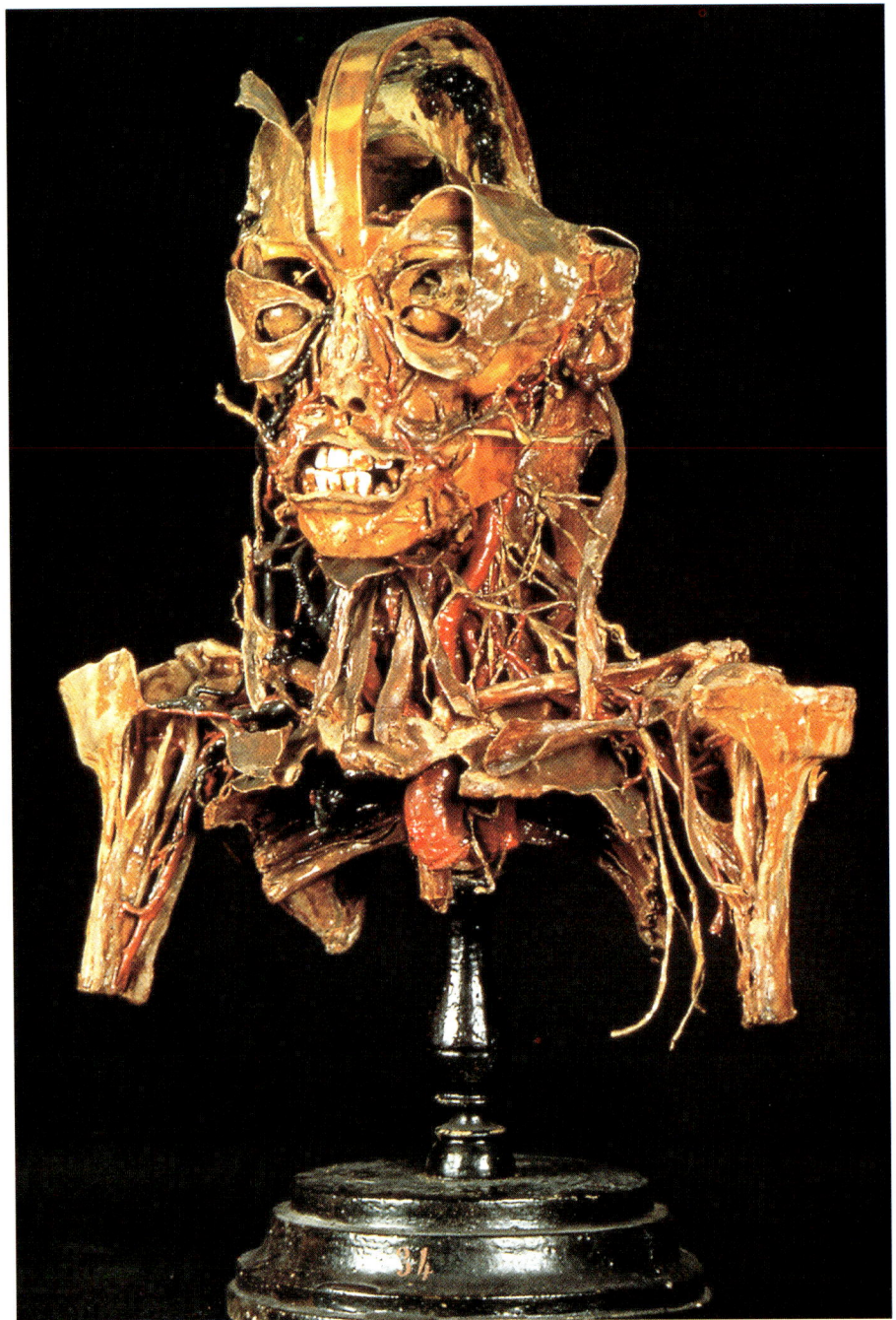

A wild imagination spurs a galloping horse.

Veterinary School, he was later accused of distorting the anatomy project and was treated as a deranged person.

Crazy he may have been, this professor obsessed with the development of scientific thought in this period of revolutionary upheavals. Or wild about new techniques: He developed a system of injections using different pressures for veins and arteries and conservation techniques that no one has been able to reproduce to this day. Or perhaps entranced with a strange aesthetic that even surpassed morbidity, by exploring flesh and its intertwined elements to transform them and challenge eternity.

A rumor at the time also claimed that he immortalized the body of his own fiancée as the horseman of the Apocalypse. Although he was a disturbing, troubled genius and was "skinned alive" by his contemporaries, he was most certainly an astonishing artist.

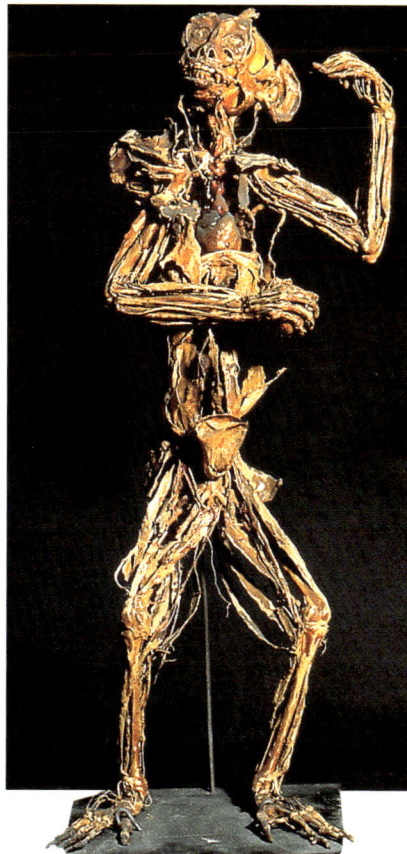

Fragonard's works reveal the complexity of human and animal bodies, but above all, they reveal the imaginary and intimate universe of the anatomist. His visions are unique, strange, and even disturbing. He was often inspired by well-known paintings, such as The Horseman of the Apocalypse, by Dürer (above); sometimes he created odd forms and busts, such as the human head (far left), in which the skull has been reduced to a circle, or a small monkey (left).

THE EXTERNAL FORM HIDES THE INNER

Vertebrae hide their essential characteristic under the mantle of their species. They all fall into the same classification, because regardless of the differences on the outside—balls of fur or sinuous scales—and variations in their habitat or behavior, they all possess a skeleton. Yet the structure of the skeleton is not always easy to detect. The clothes make the man, they say, and with animals it's the same. We judge by the external appearance of living creatures, overlooking the basic structure on which we all depend. What would be the outer form without the frame that holds together flesh, muscles, and tendons, allowing movement and support? Remove the scaffolding and everything collapses. Lines lose their shape, physical abilities disappear. These fish would lose their characteristic frowns without their enormous bony lips. And how could the jerboa jump without its oversized metatarsal bones? The skeleton determines the volumes and shapes of the body surrounding it, but it also determines its physical capacities.

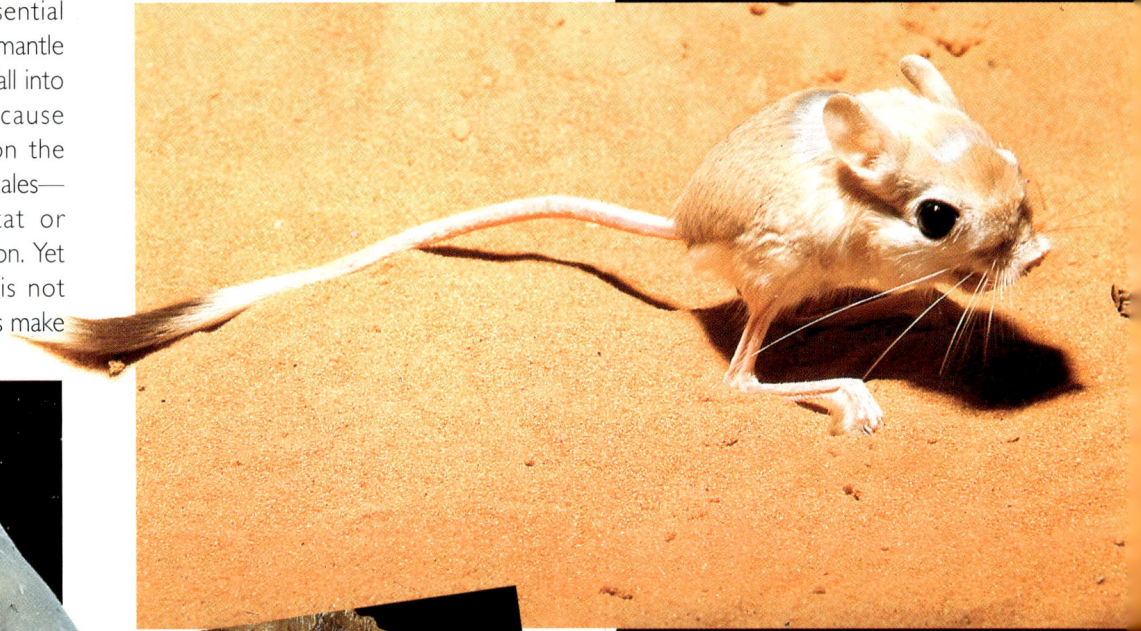

The carp has a protruding, toothless mouth surrounded by barbels, like all fish in the family Cyprinidae. It has some additional unusual anatomical features: The teeth are on the floor of the pharnax, not in the jaws. The carp grinds food against a hard pad on the lower part of the skull. They have never been highly prized in North America, partly because they are such bony fish. In Asia and Europe, however, carp are widely fished for food.

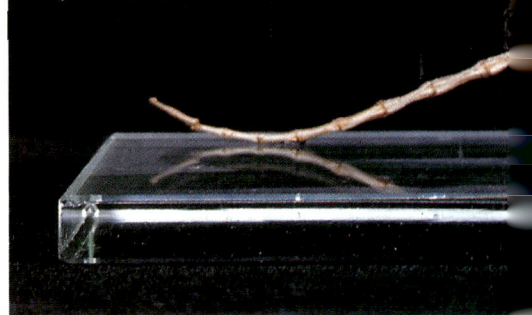

The jerboa, a small rodent that lives in the arid regions of central Asia, has the wide eyes of a nocturnal animal and immense ears, typical of desert mammals. The very long tail, longer even than the body, ends in a small tuft of white and brown bristles. It moves chiefly by jumping; the distances it moves are gigantic in relation to its small size. It measures two to six inches in length, yet can jump more than eight feet at a bound!

What makes a jerboa a champion long jumper? Its marvelous hind legs, four times longer than the front legs. The lower third of the back legs pushes off the ground to increase its spring. This power propels the jerboa to incredible speeds of up to 24 mph over short distances. The tail, ornamental on the ground, plays an essential role during the leap: It keeps the animal in balance and helps in steering. The front legs serve no special purpose in these leaps. They are used for more traditional, yet equally essential, tasks, such as searching for food and digging tunnels. Jerboa hibernate during the winter, in burrows as deep as six feet underground.

IN PRAISE OF THE HOLLOW

A bone is meant to be solid, but certainly not heavy. It shouldn't break under its own weight, like a roof beam that splits under its load. The material of the bone is organized in the most efficient way possible, with empty spaces in some areas and reinforcements elsewhere. The hollow spaces and solid pieces are distributed to provide a maximum strength for a minimum weight. The bone is a masterpiece of design that meets difficult structural requirements.

As a bone grows, it follows a subtle construction plan to solve a difficult challenge: It must remain lightweight yet provide sufficient strength to support the body. There is only one solution: to optimize the stress lines distributed along its length by creating bone tissue along the points of maximum strain. The exact structure depends on the shape, size, and function of a particular bone. The interior of a bone may be dense or tubular, ribbed or weavelike. By compensating for the forces of compression and traction, the bone manages to increase in size while reducing its weight—and all without breaking.

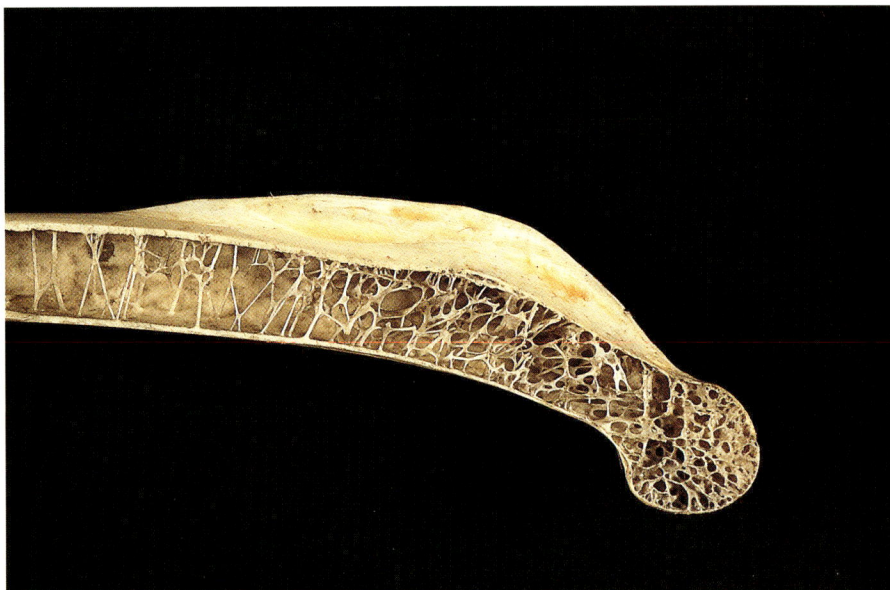

There is a bone for every purpose. It's impossible to find two bones that have solved their structural constraints in the same way. Each has an individual design according to its size, its purposes, and its limitations. Hollow spaces predominate in bird skeletons, but these bones are extremely strong due to a system of intercrossed space, such as in the swam humerus (above). The cassowary pelvis bone (opposite) reveals a regularly alternating inner structure.

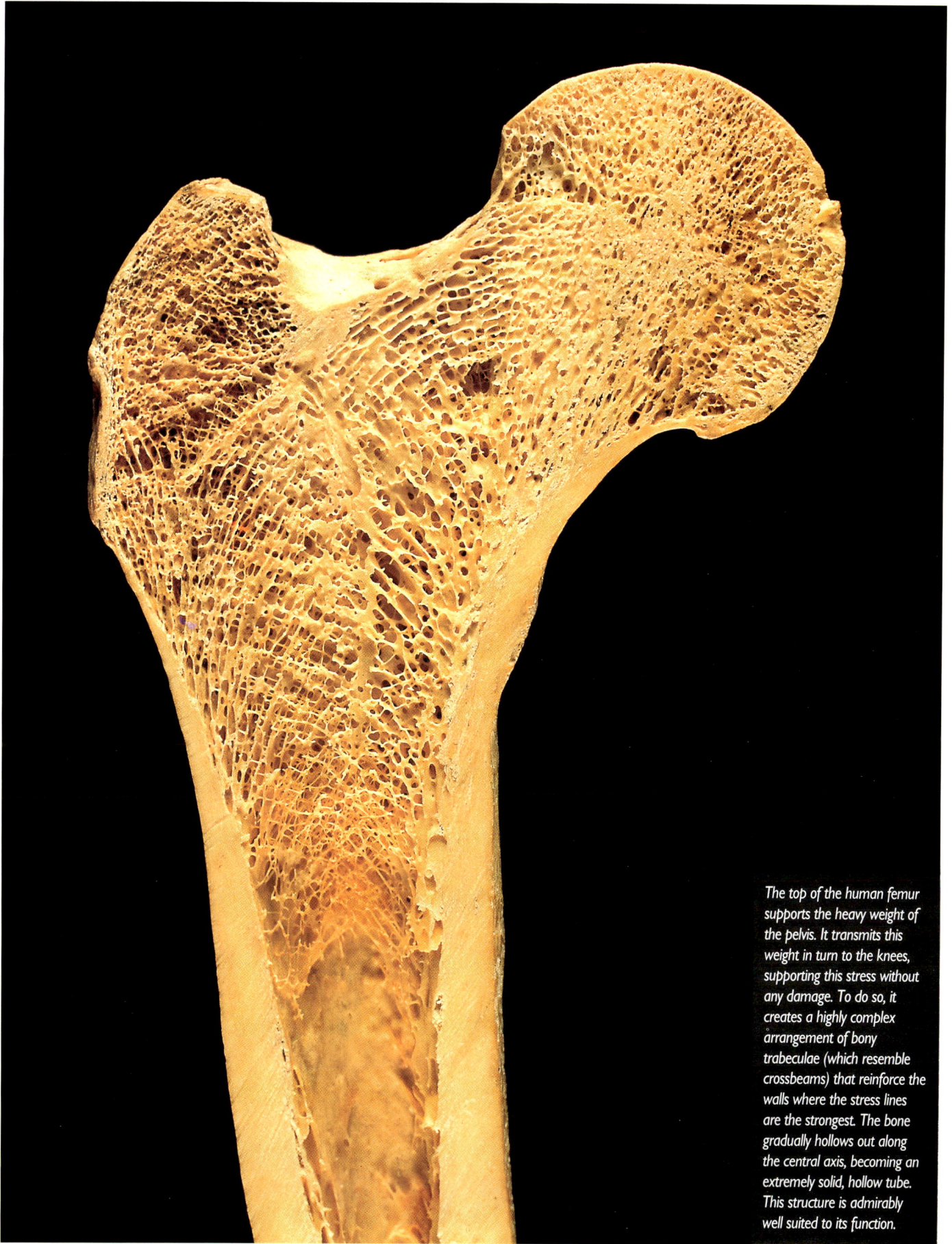

The top of the human femur supports the heavy weight of the pelvis. It transmits this weight in turn to the knees, supporting this stress without any damage. To do so, it creates a highly complex arrangement of bony trabeculae (which resemble crossbeams) that reinforce the walls where the stress lines are the strongest. The bone gradually hollows out along the central axis, becoming an extremely solid, hollow tube. This structure is admirably well suited to its function.

REASONS OF THE HEART

The intimate and mysterious secrets of phyllotaxy, or the arrangement of leaves on a stem, remains a fascinating subject for botanists. Curiously enough, physicists and mathematicians have also turned their attention to this field. These arrangements obey particular laws, which determine the order of branch growth on a tree, the complex pattern of scales on a pine cone, and the shape of flowers. What is the nature of this hidden order? It all begins with the meristems, tissues that generate the other tissues of vegetal organs and that impose strict limitations on their possible structures. The helix is one of the most sophisticated of the basic growth models. The basal meristem of the celeriac is probably the best example. The leaves appear successively around this plant, one by one, winding around the others as they grow. Each new leaf fits in between the two preceding leaves, pushing them to create enough space to grow. This stacking of leaves corresponds to two spirals, which are superimposed one on top of the other. The astonishing aspect of this type of growth pattern is that it obeys a rule, in which the number of turns in the spiral and the number of leaves are the terms of a well-known mathematical sequence, called the Fibonacci sequence (each element is the sum of its two predecessors: 1, 1, 2, 3, 5, 8, 13, and so on). This law effectively describes the growth models of plants. All types of observable spirals, in which the turns are more or less compressed—such as the red cabbage, for example—are merely variations on the arrangement of celeriac leaves. The plant's only problem is how to arrange its leaves in the least possible space, but for us, it opens up a realm of questions. Is nature governed by mathematical sequences?

A new scientific discipline may soon appear: the study of plant spirals. Its purpose? To better understand why and how these remarkable spiral structures are created by plants. Experiments and digital simulations are now being conducted in physics laboratories to clarify the mechanism of this spontaneous organization.

Just like perfectly designed mechanical gears that fit together without a fraction of an inch of play, or like the aperture of a camera, celeriac leaves overlap and interpenetrate in a clear pattern. They obey a precise mathematical law, also called the golden section. This geometric formula, which has fascinated mystics and is the basis of modern graphic design, is demonstrated in the simple growth of the celeriac.

Plants grow according to

a fascinating mathematical formula!

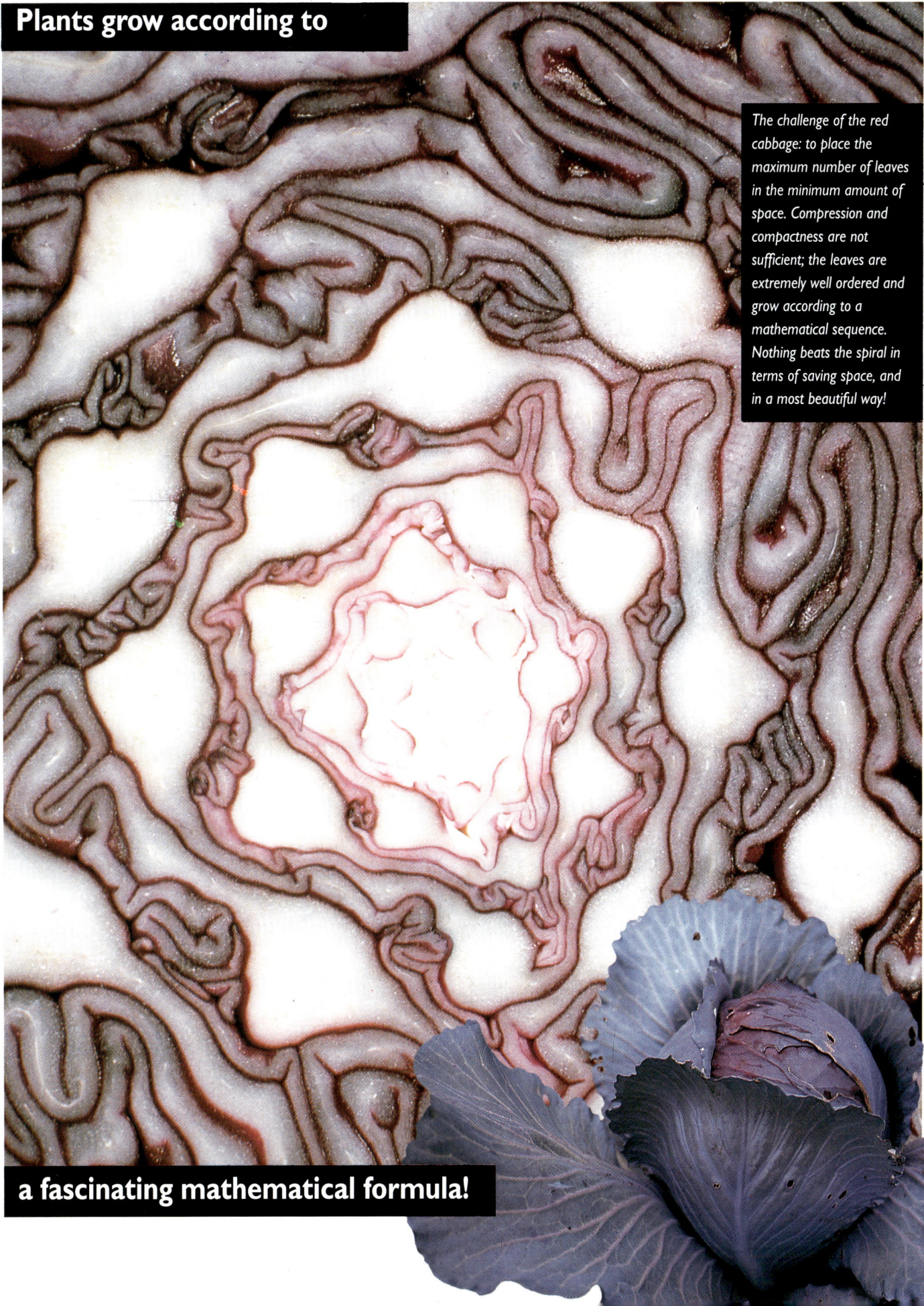

INSIDE THE SHELL, THE SPIRAL

The astonishing structure of the spiral, a marvel of mathematical order and beauty, is found everywhere in nature. What is the mystery of this repetition? Why is this shape so often repeated? Are the laws governing the growth of certain plants immutable, and is nature subject to these limits? Yes and no. The real reason is that nature has discovered the best solution within the constraints imposed by various external factors. Who or what imposed these limits? Space, the overriding

expands its home while retaining its shape and layout. From compartment to compartment, the volume increases while the structure remains identical. How does this process happen? The method is deceptively simple. The external surface must increase faster than the internal surface, in relation to the axis. The larger surface inevitably wraps around the smaller one. This is the way in which marine animals living in shells create perfect spirals.

This large shell, with its spiral form and tiger stripes, might lead us to believe that its inhabitant is just as big. False: The animal only takes up half the space. The nautilus alveolus, a mollusk cepalophode, is a clever architect and a master of design. But look at the cross section—the spiral. Why is it so perfect?

The nautilus conceals

consideration that determines shape. Every object, in developing its own form, pays its dues to space. This being the case, why not do it in the cleverest possible way, according to mathematical laws, and with an extraordinary elegance? The result is the spiral, a particularly beautiful shape when constructed by shellfish. Yet these animals do not create a simple spiral: With each twirl the shell grows larger because the animal it houses grows and needs a larger space to accommodate its larger size. The solution is a brilliant demonstration of mathematical precision. The shell grows according to a logarithmic equation. It

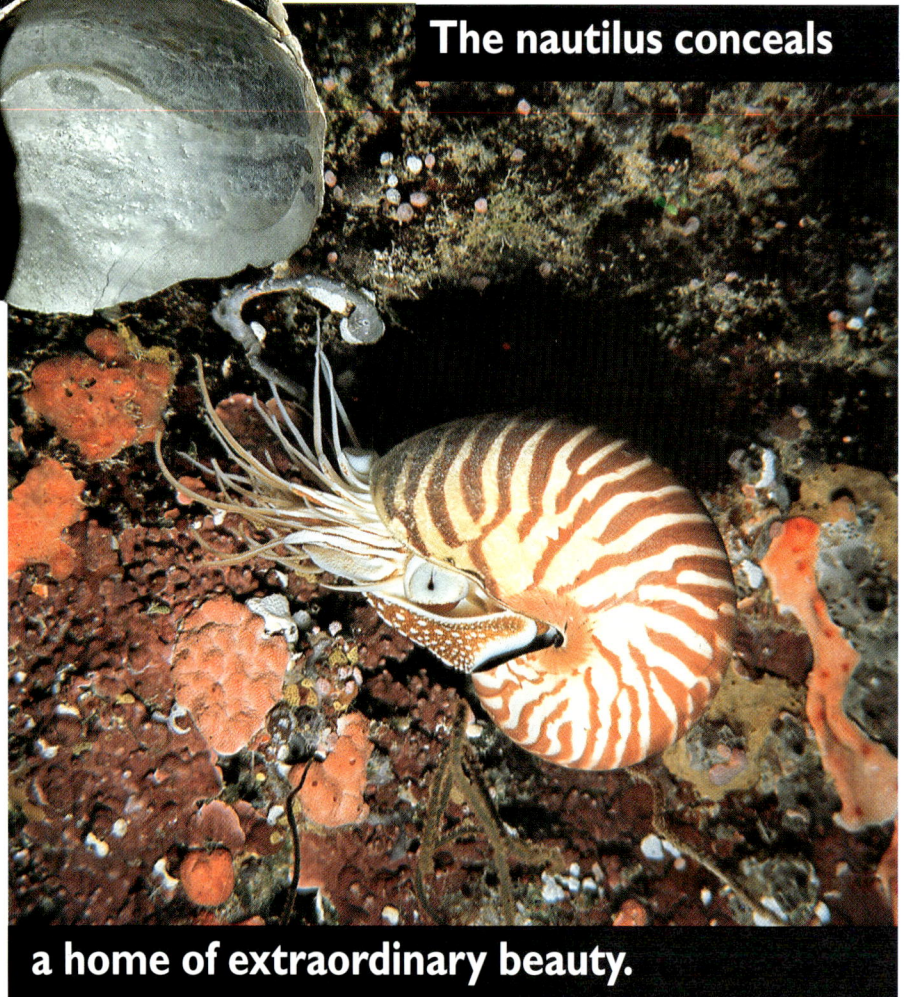

a home of extraordinary beauty.

Top: A cross section of the shells of two gastropods, the Turitula (left) and the Mitra (right), confirm the rule: To increase the volume and preserve the original structure, the growth must be faster on the outer surface than on the inner surface.

Bottom: The spiral, a three-dimensional helix, is the best possible shape for certain spatial constraints. These constraints may not be visible at first sight, but nature's forms reveal them, although secrets remain: Why do spirals always wind counterclockwise in nature and not clockwise?

DELIGHTFUL VESSELS

The plant world overflows with imagination, especially fruits, which are capable of aesthetic creations that are envied by jewelers and goldsmiths alike. Admittedly, they are receptacles for the most precious treasure of the plant: the seed, the key element in the reproductive cycle. Fruits are metamorphosed into chalices, ciboria, cupels, patellae, patens, and other archaic and artistic vessels, including cases, boxes, and finely shaped pendants. The repertory of plant finery is rich and strange: Capsules and pods have been copied by artists and jewelers. And yet beauty is not a plant's primary concern. Other requirements are more important, notably the capacity to disseminate the seeds. Although seeds must be stored under proper conditions, they must also be liberated at the right moment. The ingenuity of fruits—which remain carefully closed, bursting open spontaneously at maturity to deliver forth their contents—is nothing short of spectacular. The upper section of the fruit of the scarlet pimpernel, for example, opens up like a cover, in a generous gesture of offering. The poppy's method is astonishingly clever: The fruit is a capsule. The upper wall of this capsule, which had previously been adhered to the top, separates slightly. A small series of holes then appears, through which small bunches of seeds escape, to be carried off by the breeze. The tricks of the plant world to ensure procreation are many indeed.

The marvelous inventiveness demonstrated by fruits to store seeds has always been admired by people and has even inspired their imaginations. The fruit of the winter cherry (top), called calyxes, resembles a miniature lantern. The clever design of the poppy fruit (center) was the inspiration for salt shakers with perforated tops. Jewel boxes and certain small sacred boxes were called pix in honor of the delicacy of certain pyxidium fruits.

Right: Like all the plants in the Datura genus (Solanaceae or nightshade family), the common jimsonweed has one of the most poisonous flowers. Do the spines on the fruit serve to warn predators of its toxicity? Or do they provide better protection for the seeds?

THE ARUM'S HIDEOUT

In love, you must be clever . . .

The world would be incomplete without a little of everything . . . such as vegetation. There is an infinite variety of colors and forms, and many ways that lead to the hidden plans of all living

organisms: reproduction. The tulip, like the majority of its fellow species, proudly and shamelessly exposes its sexual organs to all. In the 17th century, while the discovery of plant reproduction was in its early stages, the tulip's bold display of sexuality was considered scandalous. But some plants evolved that hid their sex organs: the arum lily conceals such organs. Please note: He has more than a tower in his leafy folds.

The arum is a large and beautiful flower, one of the most common in the forest. It blossoms in May, long after the spear-shaped leaves have appeared, which are often spotted with a rust color. An immense pale green cone surrounds a long, dark red growth that is closed at the bottom with a curious sort of swelling. Where are the stamen? Where is the pistil? At first sight, there's nothing visible to suggest that this flower is equipped with sexual organs allowing it to reproduce! And yet not only does it possess male and female organs, but it has a fairly turbulent sex life! Everything takes place hidden from prying eyes, in the heart of this swelling. What exactly does it hide? Let's open it up to see. Here lie the stamen, bursting with compact yellow pollen, located just below a sort of hairy beard. The white and swollen ovaries, just below this complex structure, are covered with insects. Who are these unexpected guests? Small gnats, known as psikoda. They love strong smells, especially the fragrance of the arum. They pay dearly for this attraction: Drawn to the flower, they slide down the sides of the cone and are imprisoned! They are trapped and condemned to remain three days in this dark enclosure. If they attempt to escape, the network of hair acts as a trap and bars their route. As they struggle, they achieve the arum's goal, which is the fusion of the sexual organs, ensuring its reproduction. The insects are essential to the arum because the flower has a complex problem. The pollen and ovaries do not mature at the same time; therefore, the plant attracts the psikoda into its intimate hideout. At the end of their three days of imprisonment, they are released, covered with pollen, and fly from plant to plant, transferring the pollen as they go. Because of this unintended assistance, bunches of beautiful and small, but terribly poisonous orange berries appear on the branches during August. The arum provides an interesting erotic chapter in the hidden life of plants. By the way, an old custom calls for wedding sheaves to be made of arums!

or have secret weapons.

Damp walls, violent and terrifyingly slippery slopes, a suffocating heat, disturbing darkness, and a sticky powder: The small psikoda have a great deal of difficulty escaping this horrible hideout, much to the benefit of the wily arum.

LIGHT ENCASED IN MATTER

When terrible convulsions were forming the earth and when still-liquid rocks flowed like rivers, elements were in a constant state of transformation. The results are visible today in pure works of art with fascinating flashes of light: crystals, unchanging relics of nature's upsets.

How deceptive! This rock looks like a spherical or oval mass, fairly homogenous on the surface and rather dark, with no mystery whatsoever. Right? Wrong. Break it open to make an astonishing discovery. It is hollow and lined with crystals! This is a geode, a hermetically closed natural cavity, carefully protecting the fruits of its secret alchemy. Where do these unexpected jewels come from? Inside the geode, nature has created beautiful and hidden displays of multicolored crystals. Differences in temperature, pressure, and mineral composition all combined to form these treasures. Initially, gas bubbles of various sizes were trapped within a flow of molten basalt. As it cooled and hardened, the volatile elements could no longer escape, and the bubbles were trapped in the cooling mass. Cavities were formed, but they were not completely empty. Hot solutions containing various minerals were still circulating in the cavity; they crystalized as they cooled. Crystals, which sometimes cover the walls of a geode, develop toward its center. Some geodes are hollow.

Basalt is profoundly altered in hot climates, and geodes sometimes stand out from their rocky surroundings. The quartz geode (above) was found in Morocco; the agate (below), composed of goethite and quartz crystals, came from Mexico.

Open a geode to discover

its hidden pearls.

Rhodochrosite forms an eternal flame. These one-inch long crystals, trapped in a matrix of black quartz and mixed with balls of white calcite, illuminate the inside of a Mexican geode.

THE FILM OF TIME

Time: Measure it, cut it up, and break it into pieces to regulate it, or even better, to dominate it. Time is one of man's oldest preoccupations. Ancient scientists worked hard to "invent" time, a straightforward, dependable time, unrelated to the lunar cycles of the rotation of the sun. They were looking for an invariable, tamed, calculated, redefined, artificial, and autonomous notion of time. Furthermore, one that was exact. Time has subtly, inexorably taken over our lives and is the silent drumbeat that controls the rhythm of our daily schedules. For years, everyone has carried a piece of time imprisoned in tiny cases and strapped to a wrist or worn around the neck. Now, however, electronic technology has banished the uncertainty of ticking springs, blades, and other mechanical elements. These tiny gears have been replaced by electronic circuits; the pendulum is now a quartz crystal, and the battery has replaced the wind-up stem. Technology has gone straight to the heart of time: It vibrates to the rhythm of crystal pulses, in millions of tiny movements per second. Yet despite these developments and technological transformations, time still preciously guards its meaning behind its own "language." It is always passing, slipping away, lost, found, gained, caught up, beaten, and regretted. It moves too slowly, too fast, and is, ultimately, irreversible.

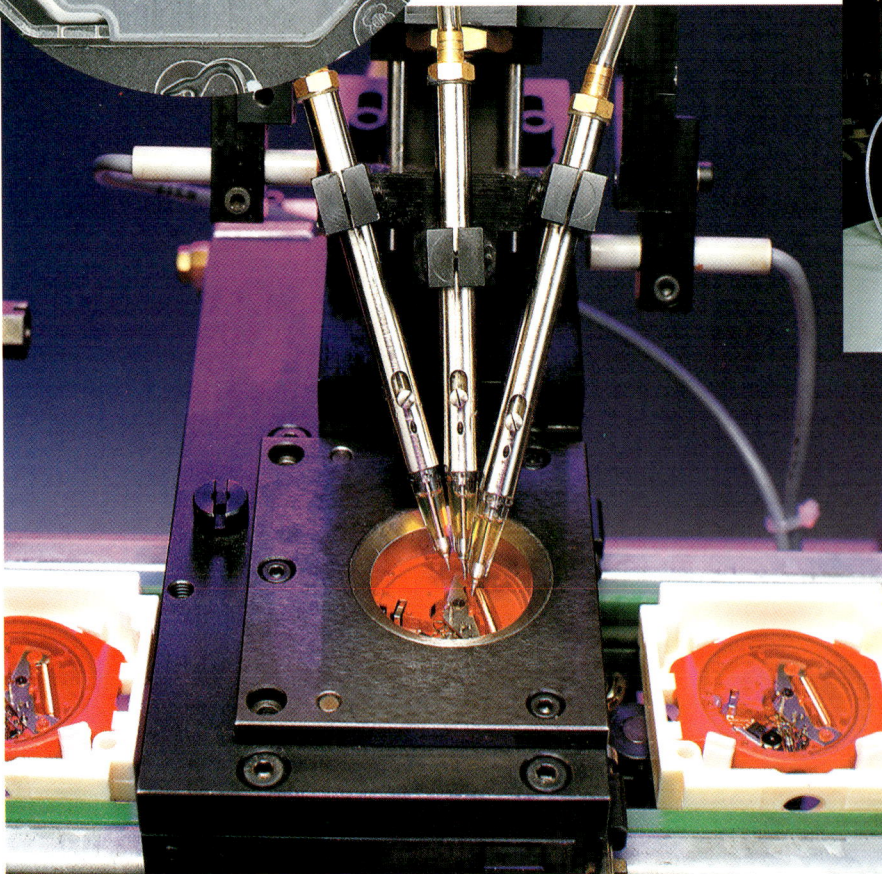

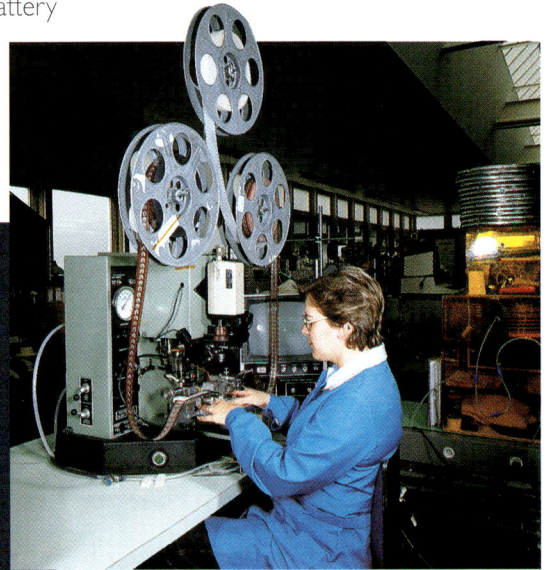

The electronic modules used in the Swiss Swatch watches are printed on film. They are first cut out one by one, then welded directly in the watch case by a robot on the assembly line. This type of watch has a limited life span and cannot be replaced.

Old-fashioned clockworks are fascinating mechanical pieces, yet modern movements have their own special beauty. The film of time unfolds like an old-fashioned movie.

Beyond appearances

The world turns its back on us. We are allowed to see only the external appearance of objects or beings. Throughout history, mankind has been condemned to a "skin-deep" view of the surrounding world. But a change in strategy, combined with technological advances, has at long last broken through to the mysteries beyond.

Inside the soft exterior lies the hard inner structure: white the hard element, black the softer one. Through the magic of X rays, the body of this Amazonian lizard becomes transparent and reveals the bony skeleton within. This exploration is as amazing as that of the diver, who penetrates the earth's skin under the polar cap to see the underside of the world.

TRANSPARENT METAL

By nature, metal is opaque and reveals nothing of its inner depths. Yet its secrets cannot withstand the powerful eyes of technology. Radiography has given us the means to see through the opaque surface to the inner structure: X rays probe the invisible, and the mysteries of Tibetan and Merovingian art are revealed.

God or demon of the Himalayas, this Bodhisattva Vajrapani has been identified as a 12th-century Tibetan copy of an original work created in the 11th century. How can art historians be so certain and exact in their assessment? X-ray examinations revealed that the metal of this statuette was cast around a central core, supported from the tiara to the feet by a metal armature.

This internal structure gives the beautiful grace to this piece by immortalizing movement in metal. The talent of the craftsman can be seen by examining the walls, which are thin and regular. The small opaque spots on the lower and upper members, however, reveal places that had to be filled in later, as there was not enough brass in the original casting.

This technique also saved from oblivion a shapeless mass of no apparent interest. Although this piece was buried for a long time in damp earth and was covered with a thick coat of rust, X rays revealed that it was, in fact, a superb belt buckle made in the 7th century! A fine inlay of silver wire, hammered into a geometric pattern, was detected after discovery, leading to its restoration. Radiographic tests can therefore provide previously unknown data, without any harm to the original work. It is a precious tool used to acquire evidence to support historic and artistic theories and to reveal the concealed beauty of a seemingly uninteresting work. Sacred statuettes and magnificent clothing accessories can still reveal surprises, even across centuries of neglect.

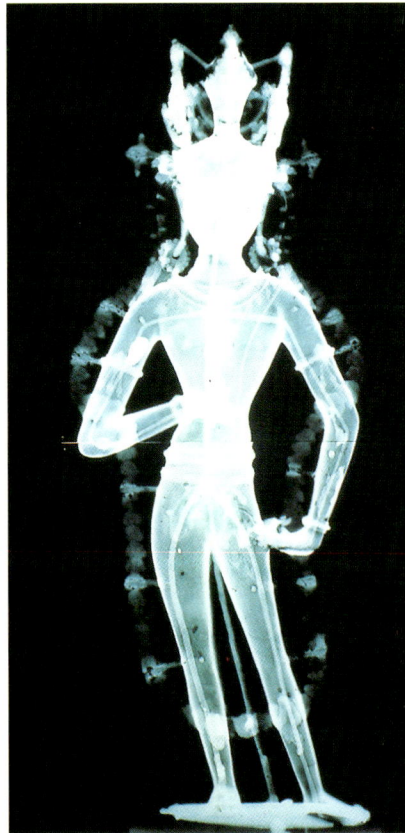

The penetration of X rays is determined by their wavelength and by the nature and density of the material tested. Any difference in thickness (or of chemical composition) is immediately visualized. The lighter areas designate a high density, while empty sections appear darker. Under the piercing view of X-ray technology, the sculptural talents of the artist are brought to light.

Behind the Tibetan god hides a being of light and contrast. The metal armature—formed of four quadrangular rods (one vertical, one across, and two for the legs)—the rivets and areas that were subsequently touched up all appear in the X ray. A god, who only recently revealed his age, his origins, and his inner being!

The three elements of the Merovingian belt buckle are revealed: the back plate, the reinforcing plate, and the loop plate, with bronze nails for attaching the leather. The inlaid work (or damascening) and the shapes date this loop. It even reveals whether the owner was a man or a woman!

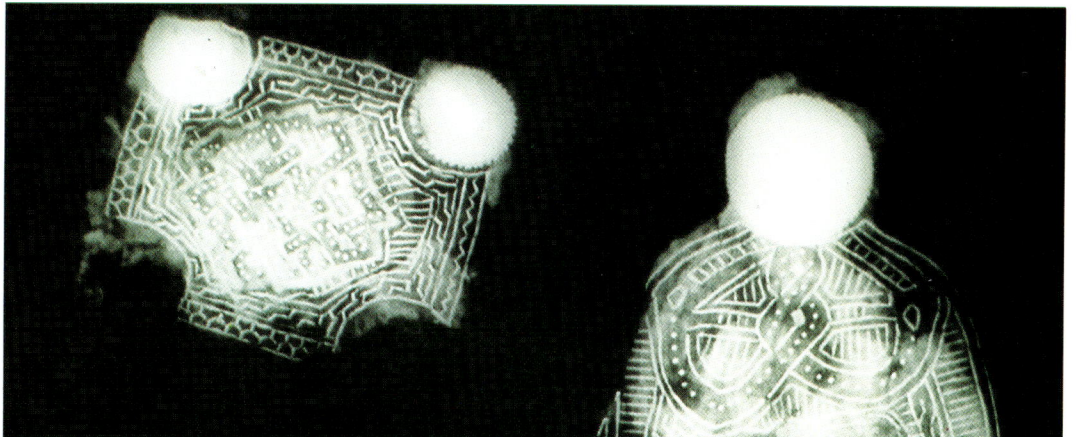

Under a shapeless mass, a precious buckle

ART UNMASKED

Art and science: a fascinating encounter, where researchers become investigators and works are seen as coded messages. Radiography is one of the most valuable tools used by these art detectives. An X-ray image of a painting reveals the inner structure of the work. It is a black-and-white image, of course, but the range of subtleties is so vast that it almost rivals the colorful surface. Suddenly, the many questions concerning the techniques of a certain painting, its physical condition, and its origins can be answered. These

answers are sometimes surprising. Detective work can have unexpected results, and many works have had to be reevaluated in the light of new information. Scanning the photograph provided by the X-ray examination, the eye of the technician penetrates under the painted surface. He first determines the nature of the support, which is generally a wood frame over which a linen canvas is stretched. He then discovers the substance used to prime the canvas, which prepares it for the subsequent layers of paint. This is highly

revealing. Certain preparations were common at one time and place and not another; many imitations can therefore be detected at this stage. Pigments, binders, and varnishes are then analyzed; these techniques are difficult for a copyist to discover and duplicate. Every chemical element absorbs X rays in a different way and reflects different levels of gray. Aside from answering questions concerning the authenticity of a particular work, X rays can also reveal the technique used by the artist to create effects of light and shadows and the interaction of colors. Even better, it can reveal the secrets of the composition and can detect preparatory sketches, areas where the artist may have changed his mind and corrected the composition.

Behind one painting often lies another.

What new information will the researcher discover by comparing the X-ray photograph of a nativity with the smooth surface and serene happiness depicted in the original painting? With the penetrating vision of the X-ray technique, he can visualize the homogeneity of the pictorial layer, along with any missing areas and overpainting. The painter's process is revealed to a fascinated contemporary viewer.

An X-ray photograph leaves the material of the painting untouched, but it may seriously alter contemporary consideration of the work. These images are sometimes cruel to the artist, who has often taken great care to conceal any hesitations, errors, or alterations. These are all brought to light and demystified by the unforgiving rays. Each sketch and line, even those covered by a thick layer of paint, are analyzed on the screen and offered to the view of fascinated and enchanted art historians.

An enigmatic figure clothed in light. This is not a religious vision; it is a statuette, which has suffered severely over time and is in serious need of a complete physical examination. The "archaeologist-doctor" has a difficult task at hand: to understand the mechanisms of deterioration and to make a diagnosis before starting any restoration. She can use the X-ray photograph to detect any alterations and to determine the necessary treatment.

THE PLAY OF ICE

The expression "cold as ice" describes the attitude of a person who cannot be budged, shocked, or shaken. This description of ice is anything but accurate! To use ice as a metaphor for immobility is a great mistake; ice, in fact, is active and moves in great sweeping movements. It never stops moving and changing shape. We can see the evidence of its vital energy in the geologic traces left from the ice age and in the polar cap of today. Close to 11% of the continental earth's surface (which represents no less than 6 million square miles) is covered by glaciers, and a quarter of the world's water contains floating icebergs. And this is only the beginning because 15,000 years remain in this glacial era, and more and more ice will form during these millennia. And meanwhile, everything is in motion! Glaciers grow and recede. The level of the sea is constantly changing. The two phenomena are intimately linked: When the global glacier cover increases, the overall level of the oceans drops; it rises again as the glaciers retreat. All this activity takes place, of course, on the scale of geologic time, but if we were not limited to our ephemeral human condition, we could see the earth bury or raise up continental blocks as a reaction to the successive pressures of moving ice. In other words, we could almost see the planet's breath. Despite their unmoving appearance, glaciers are highly active. They increase and decrease in volume, gain or lose ground, and advance or retreat their leading edge. Furthermore, they reproduce! This "calving" occurs when blocks of ice break loose from the main glacier, creating icebergs, which then drift with the winds and the tide. Certain glaciers in Antarctica release close to 150 million tons of ice per day. Icebergs, formed from ice several thousands of years old, can survive for 10 years and travel more than 1,250 miles. The evolution of glaciers, which are subtle combinations of air and water, contains the history of the earth's atmosphere. Core borings taken from glaciers provide important information concerning the composition of the atmosphere as it existed several thousand years ago.

What stories can these icy fragments

The current of Greenland in the Arctic Ocean carries 6,200 cubic miles of icebergs every year. This iceberg, with rough, jagged edges, broke free from a glacier in Alaska. It carries the scars of the constant friction of its surface with the surrounding waves.

reveal to us?

Vast crevasses can open in certain sections of glaciers (this one in Alaska), creating deep caverns in their blue depths. We can discover their history by penetrating the ice cap and breathing the frozen air.

THE HORIZONS OF THE SOIL

Would you like to see another world? Dig straight down into the ground and you will discover new horizons, those studied by pedologists, specialists in soil science. They study the various layers of the soil, its colors, and structures that change depending on the area. Pedologists have a different vision of the world. Perhaps they are tired of watching a single horizon and are drawn to the multiple worlds underground. Calcite or siliceous, sandy or humus: The offer is vast. From the surface of the parent rock, you can cross at least four other layers by following the zones of water infiltration or the accumulation of products that result from the deterioration of other layers. The dividing lines result from a multitude of factors interacting between the soil and the subsoil. An entire range of horizons emerge from the effects of water, temperature, atmosphere, wind, and life (intense and varied) and the multiple exchanges between these elements, from the mother rock to the soil.

A continual transformation from rock to soil.

Soil is a living environment, which exists in a constant state of interaction with surrounding factors. Plants enrich the soil with organic material through their roots and radicles (to the right, grass roots). A multitude of organisms inhabit this world: microorganisms, earthworms, and threadworms, and a host of insects. Larger animals also call it home, including the mole, a carnivorous creature, or the small lizards that live in desert regions (below, the bearded lizard of eastern Australia). These reptiles lay their eggs up to 20 inches deep, safe from the extreme variations in temperature between day and night.

The nature of the parent rock, which gradually produces soil, can be determined by using a geologic technique called core sampling. Cylindrical samples, or cores, are cut from the rock by a special tool, the core barrel. Left: a crate of cores extracted from the ground in Zaire by means of a sloped core barrel.

Screens of reality

Technology is our most valuable tool in the constant quest to obtain knowledge of unknown worlds. Its sophisticated arsenal allows us to detect, probe, analyze, and calculate the tiniest piece of data, impossible to detect from our limited view. Inanimate objects (such as works of art) and animate beings (such as humans) provide the most unusual images. We must then learn how to interpret the complicated code of these images. With these screens, man reconstructs reality.

An infrared examination of this painting revealed two signatures on the clothing of the central couple that had been invisible to the naked eye. Certain painting substances become transparent under the infrared camera, so that the underlying layers of a painting can be seen.

THE COLORS OF HEAT

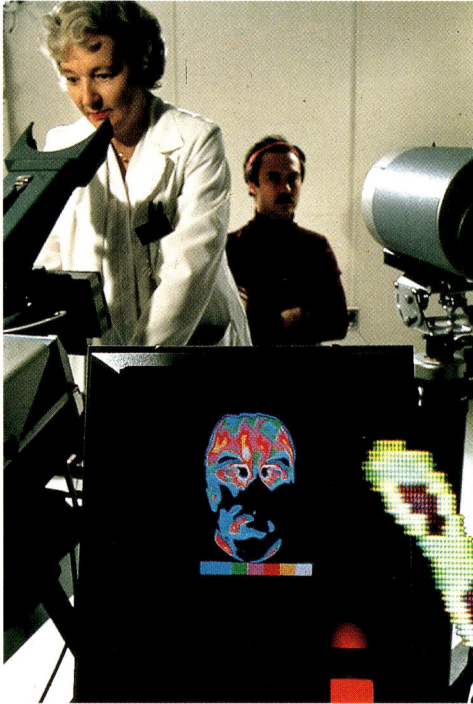

The body is sometimes an unmitigated liar. Or at best, it hides itself well. How? By revealing only its surface layer. An observer thinks he has seen all there is to see: From head to toe, the skin remains a fairly homogenous color. Yet under the opaque layer of skin the body protects a multitude of elements: flesh, muscle, organs, bone, blood. And they all have different colors! To be more precise, they all have different temperatures. The body is unmasked through the eyes of new, sophisticated equipment. This equipment considers color and heat to be one and the same thing. Thermography, a technique that detects the temperature of a given object, as its name indicates, transcribes heat into the language of color. Mixtures of liquid crystals are used in this technique; they translate the color of the different temperatures they receive. Video cameras that detect the infrared waves emitted by an object and transform them into images are also used. By measuring the temperature of a certain area of the body, we can see what is hidden underneath: Each source of heat creates a different color. The colors range across the entire spectrum: A few degrees' difference in temperature creates a color change from a brownish red to a light green, or a blue to a violet.

For doctors, the use of images obtained with thermography has little to do with aesthetics: The interest lies in the information they provide. For example, the visualization of "hot" or "cold" zones can designate areas that have too much or too little circulation. This information may be extremely important in the subsequent diagnosis of an illness.

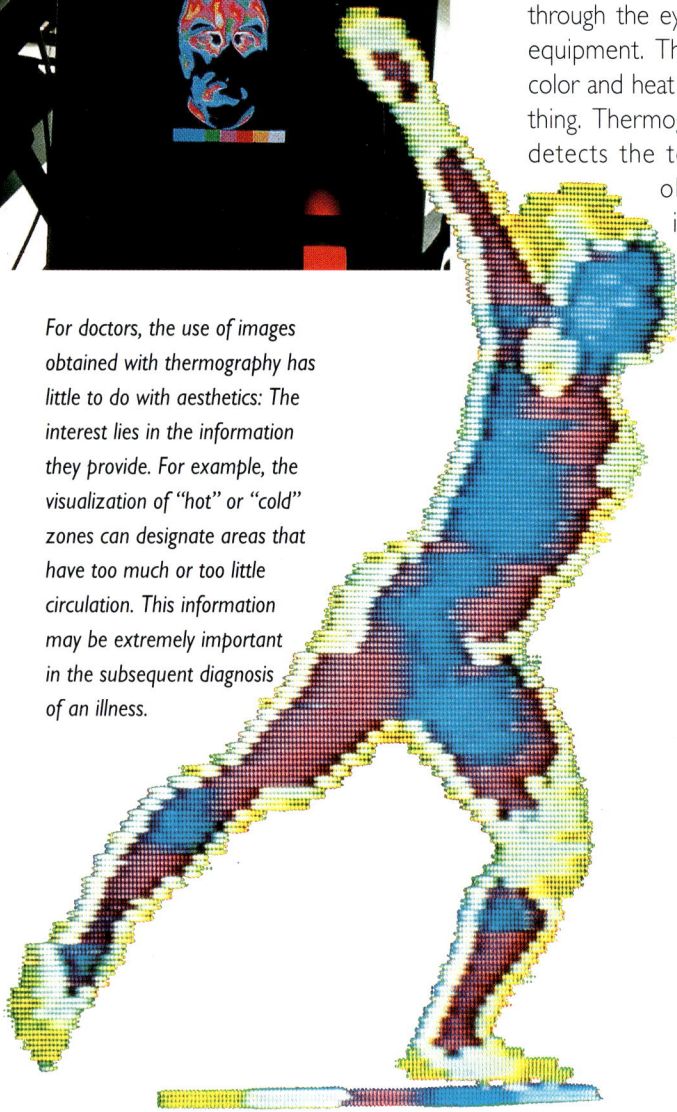

Smokers, your hands betray you:

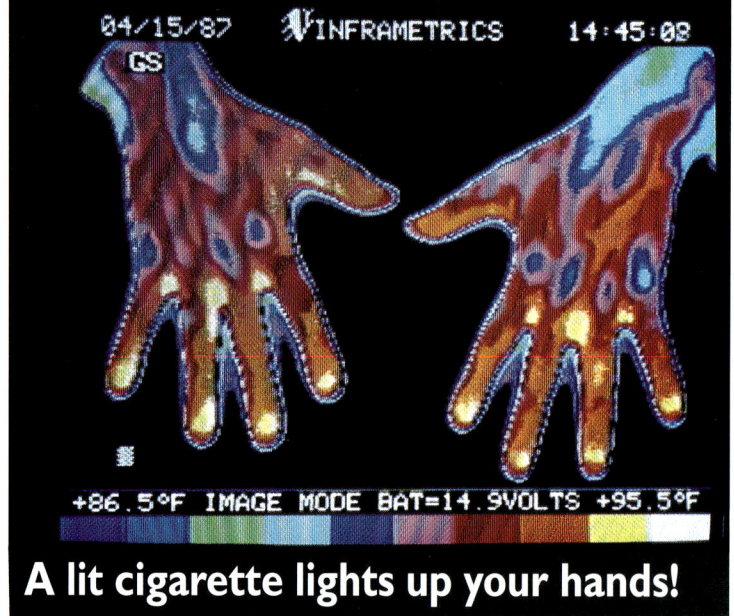

04/15/87 INFRAMETRICS 14:45:08
GS

+86.5°F IMAGE MODE BAT=14.9VOLTS +95.5°F

A lit cigarette lights up your hands!

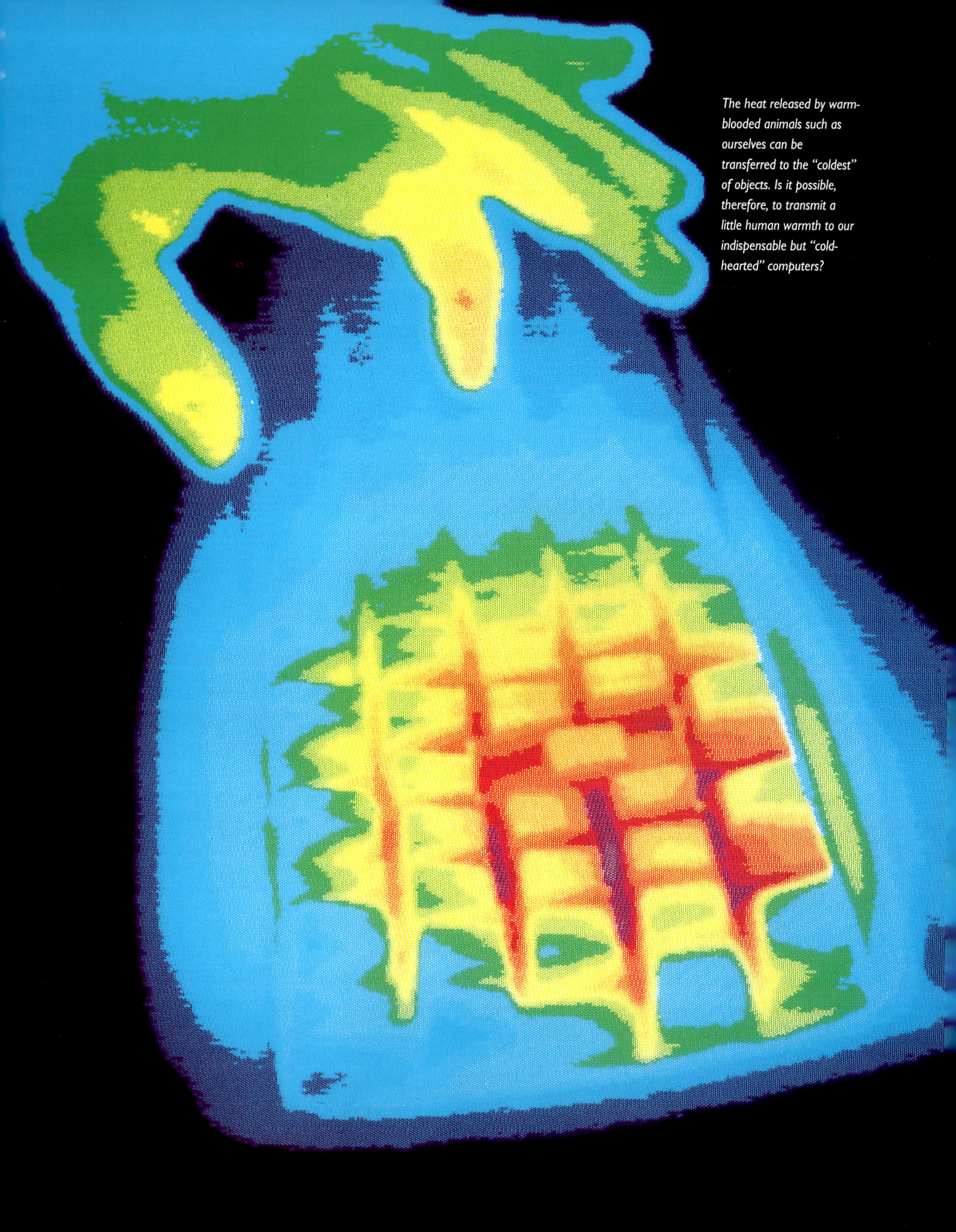

The heat released by warm-blooded animals such as ourselves can be transferred to the "coldest" of objects. Is it possible, therefore, to transmit a little human warmth to our indispensable but "cold-hearted" computers?

DANCING PROTONS

What lies behind this strange armor? Is it an extraterrestrial or some kind of mutant? No, it is just one of the best examples of medical imaging, a representation of the human body, which has been explored with the techniques of nuclear Magnetic Resonance Imaging.

It is based on the detection of molecules and particles. We are, of course, formed of molecules, which are made of atoms. Each atom has a core, which in turn contains protons, minuscule masses with a positive electrical charge.

This technique is based on the high proportion of water in our bodies: More than 85% of our brain is formed of water! Water molecules contain a particular atom, hydrogen, which has a single proton. Thanks to these protons, we can examine the inside of the human body, from head to toe. Protons are in perpetual movement. They rotate around one another and act like small magnets, forming magnetic fields. If they are subjected to a much stronger magnetic force, they vibrate and resonate at the same frequency as the received magnetic wave. This effect of resonance results in an electrical signal whose intensity is proportional to the number of protons present in the area being examined. From these signals, which are amplified, the quantity of water in a tissue can be determined. This provides information concerning its condition, whether healthy or not, once the computer has integrated and digitized all the data. The protons create an image on the screen that is an actual three-dimensional map of the organ.

The technician interprets the image of his patient's brain, displayed on the monitor in the control room where all the data obtained by the MRI is processed. This examination requires complex equipment, but it is not dangerous to the patient.

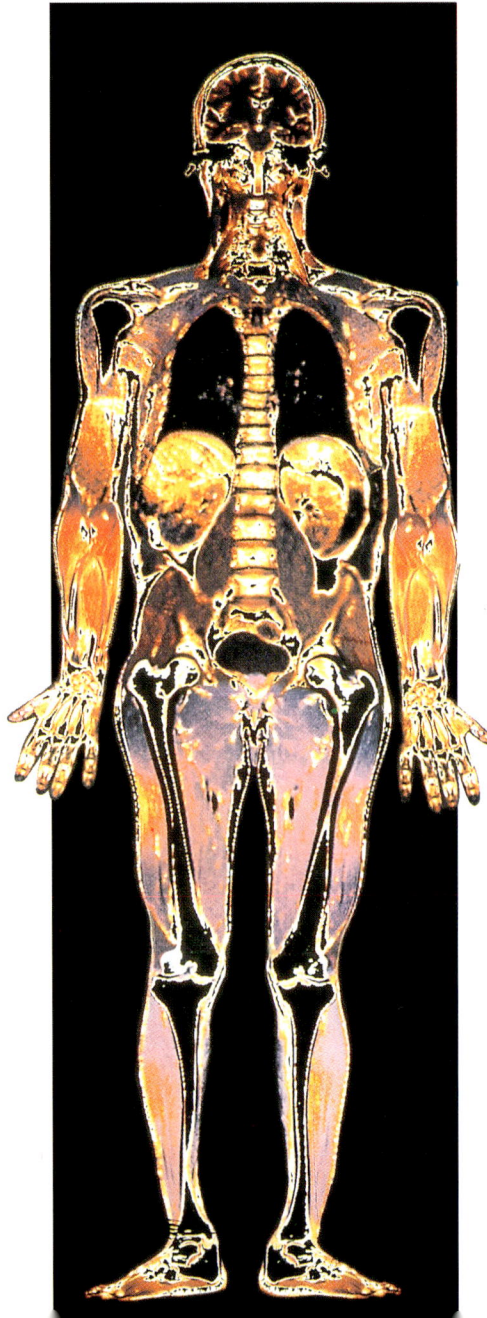

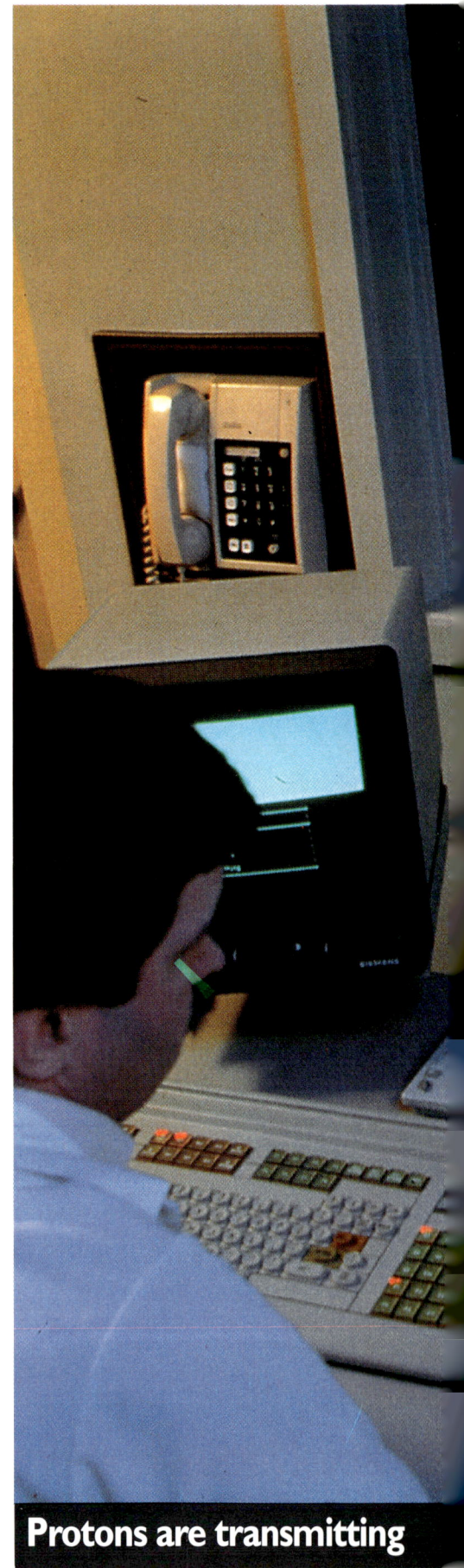

Protons are transmitting

from the core of our molecules.

A KALEIDOSCOPE OF TECHNIQUES

We are living in the era of images. Some approve, others don't. But in the field of medicine, there is no hesitation. New technologies allow us to see the body as never before. It has been divided into sectors, territories, and zones. The individual under the technological kaleidoscope is a spectacular sight indeed.

For imaging purposes, a specific piece of equipment corresponds to each tissue and each organ. The skeleton is most revealing to beams; the abdomen, however, prefers ultrasound. The brain reacts best to protons and isotopes, and skin to infrared. And, of course, X-ray photography reveals bone structure, while scintigraphy explores certain glands, and the scanner detects cerebral convolutions. What works for one area and for one type of organ does not necessarily work for others. An armada of techniques exists, along with highly trained specialists, to decode the electronic and visual results. They can no longer depend on their eyes to examine a human body that has become a surrealist landscape. These new explorers of inner space must analyze, decipher, decode, and interpret the vast array of information obtained about the human body.

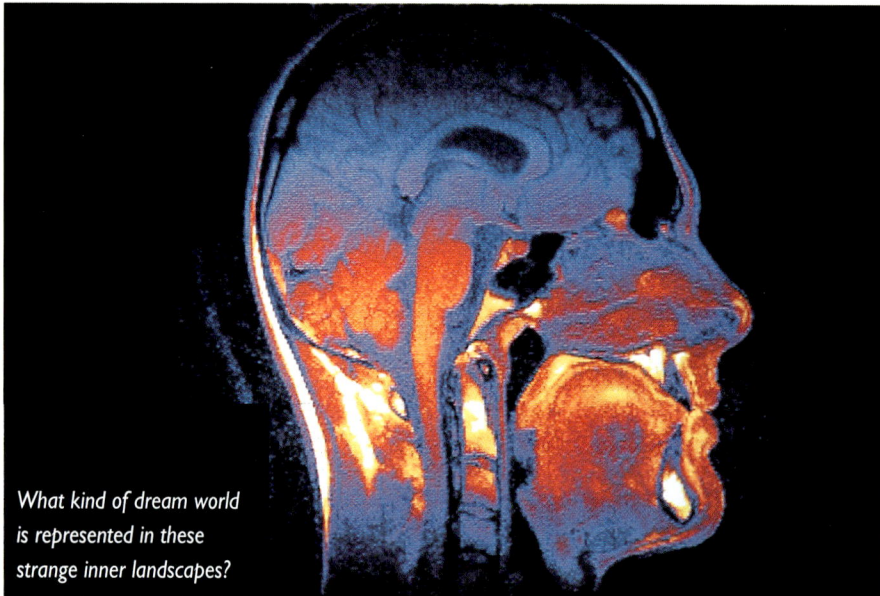

What kind of dream world is represented in these strange inner landscapes?

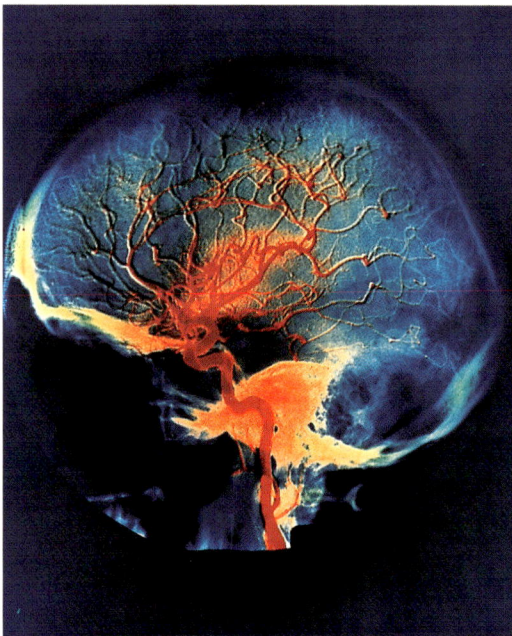

Who would believe that a prostate viewed with an ultrasonic device (below) could produce such a beautiful image, or that a brain, examined by digitized arteriography (left) could be so poetic?

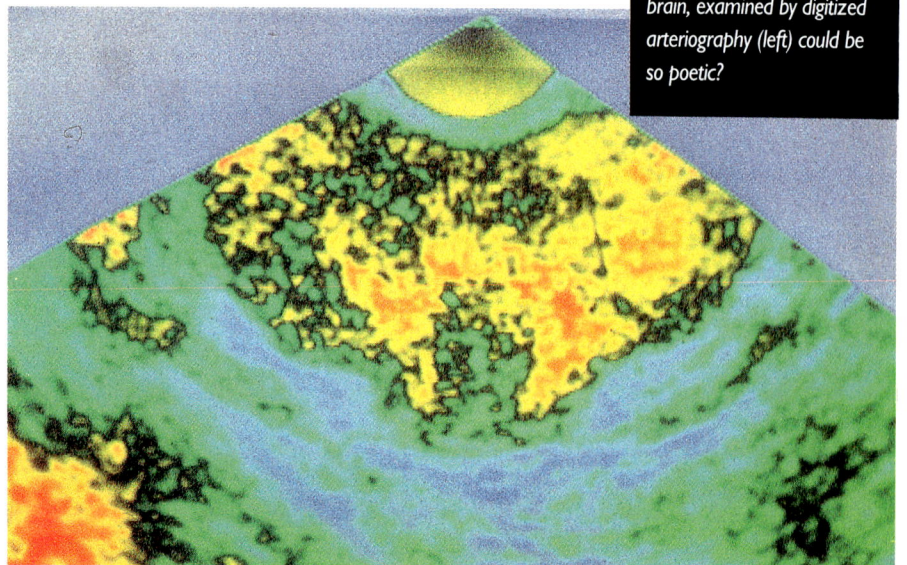

44

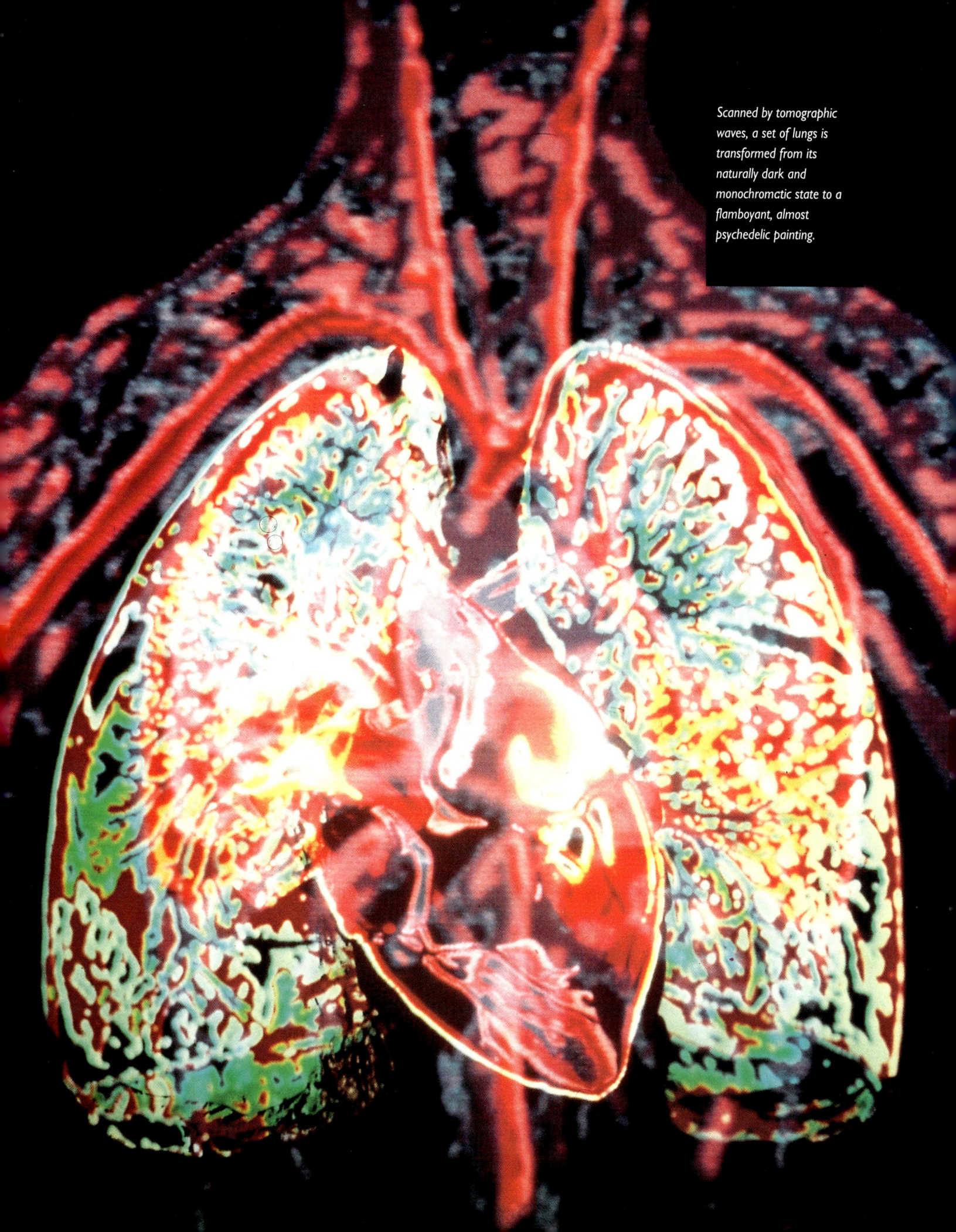

Scanned by tomographic waves, a set of lungs is transformed from its naturally dark and monochromatic state to a flamboyant, almost psychedelic painting.

VISIBLE METAMORPHOSES

Shedding skin! Escaping a rigid yoke that limits and prevents creatures from flying away to conquer new horizons. . . . A dream of such privileged beings we can only envy: those astonishing insects that can metamorphosize. Crickets, grasshoppers, dragonflies, praying mantises, phasmids, cicadas . . . they are pros at this game. Each begins its life as an unimaginative larva, slowly escaping this stage through several moltings, its skin hardening little by little. One day the larva freezes completely and becomes almost motionless—this is called a chrysalis. During this time the greatest alteration takes place: Everything dissolves, everything restructures, everything changes; and the adult imago arises. The fully developed insect emerges, dries off, and unfolds its wings. A new and unimaginable life has begun.

Right before our very eyes the nymph transforms: Hard, compact, still, dark, and oblong, the adult emerges, pale and soft. This shattering contrast brings about the unexpected. Suddenly the world itself appears to be a chrysalis of possibilities. All depends on watching what lays before us. We can be actors of metamorphosis where beings and things change from their form, their nature, and their structure and become unrecognizable. And our spirits, our dreams, our fantasies release themselves from our imaginations to enrich themselves through unknown horizons; those from a universe so close and incredibly hidden.

Photo Credits

P. 2: © Bramaz/Jerrican (top left), ©Nasa/ Ciel et Espace (top right), © Catherine Pouedras (center), © Peter Parks/ OSF, Fovéa (bottom left), © Hervé Berthoule/ Jacana (botom right). P. 3: © Patrick Dacosta. P. 4: © Paul Starosta. P. 5: © Claude Nuridsany et Marie Pérennou. P. 6: © David Thompson/ OSF, Fovéa (top), © Alain Compost/ Bios. P. 7: © Alain Compost/ Bios. P. 8 © Philippe Plally (left), © R. Konig/ Jacana. P. 9: © Claude Nuridsany et Marie Pérennou. P. 10: © Patrick Landmann. P. 11: © Patrick Landmann. P. 12: © Yoff/ Jacana (top), © P. Gathercole/ OSF, Jacana (left), © B. Faye/ MNHN (center). P. 13: © J. M. Labat/ Jacana. P. 14: © B. Faye/ MNHN. P. 15: © B. Faye/ MNHN. P. 16: © Claude Nuridsany. P. 17: © Claude Nuridsany et Marie Pérennou. P. 18: © OSF/ Oncunae, Fovéa/ Sequoia (left), © D. Faulkner/ Jacana. P. 19: © Claude Nuridsany et Marie Pérennou. P. 20: © Michel Viard/ Odyssey (top right), © Claude Nuridsany et Marie Pérennou (center), © Claude Nuridsany et Marie Pérennou (bottom), © Claude Nuridsany et Marie Pérennou (bottom). P. 21: © Michel Viard/ Odyssey. P.22: © Méro/ Jacana (left), © Marie Pérennou (right). P. 23: © Claude Nuridsany et Marie Pérennou. P. 24: © Hervé Berthoule/ Jacana (top), © Nelly Bariand (bottom). P. 25: © Nelly Bariand. P. 26: © Bramaz/ Jerrican. P. 27: © Bramaz/ Jerrican. P. 28–29: © Xavier Desmier/ CEDRI. P. 29: © J. P. Gasc. P. 30: © Musée Guimet/ Louvre. P. 31: © Musée Guimet/ Louvre. P. 32: © Labat et Viard/ Jerrican. P. 33: © Viard/ Oddyssey. P. 34: © Bean/ Sipa Press. P. 35: © Bean/ Sipa Press. P. 36: © BRGM. P. 37: © OSF/ Oncunae, Fovéa/ Séquoia (top), © Jean-Philippe Varin/ Jacana (center), © J. Weigel, ANT/NHPA (bottom). P. 38–39: © Musée du Louvre. P. 39: © Laboratoire de recherche des musées de France. P. 40: © H. Sochureck/ Cosmos (left), © Douglas B. Nelson/ Fovéa (center), © H. Sochureck/ Cosmos (right). P. 41: © Chuck O'Rear/ Cosmos. P. 42: © J. C. Révy/ CNRI. P. 43: © Zefa/ Stockmarket. P. 44: © Jean-Luc Ziegler/ Bios (top), © A. Pol/ CNRI (left), © Gomberg/ Sipa Press (right). P. 45: © H. Sochureck/ Zefa. P. 47: © Judy Davidson, Science photo library/ Cosmos. Front Cover: © B. Van Berg / Image Bank; © Jeff Rotman et Peter Arnold / Cosmos. Back Cover: © Bean / Sipa Press.

Design and layout: Etienne Hénocq - François Huertas.

New Discovery Books
Macmillan Publishing Company
866 Third Avenue
New York, NY 10022

Maxwell Macmillan Canada, Inc.
1200 Eglinton Avenue East
Suite 200
Don Mills, Ontario M3C 3N1

Macmillan Publishing Company is part of the Maxwell Communication Group of Companies.

First Edition
Printed in the United States of America
10 9 8 7 6 5 4 3 2 1

ISBN 0-02-711737-5
Library of Congress Catalog Card Number 93-9459

33575

500
BOU   Bousquet, Catherine

         Incredibly hidden

DUE DATE	BRODART	01/95	14.95